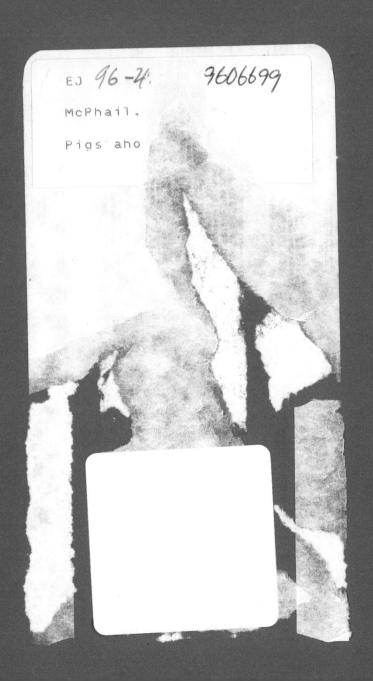

PIGS AHOY!
·····

DAVID McPHAIL

DUTTON CHILDREN'S BOOKS   NEW YORK

For Hailey—
something to read while Art is bowling

Copyright © 1995 by David McPhail

CIP Data is available.

Published in the United States 1995 by Dutton Children's Books,
a division of Penguin Books USA Inc.
375 Hudson Street, New York, New York 10014

Designed by Riki Levinson

Printed in Hong Kong   First Edition
10 9 8 7 6 5 4 3 2   ISBN 0-525-45334-2

Today I'm going on a trip.
I'll cruise the ocean on a ship.
I pack my luggage, turn the lock,
And take a taxi to the dock.

When I arrive it's nearly dark.
The ship is ready to embark.
The Captain's leaning on the rail.
I go aboard, and we set sail.

I look for cabin number nine.
To my surprise, it's filled with swine.
Some are sitting on a trunk;
The rest are piled up on a bunk.

"Come on in!" the pigs declare.
"The top bunk's yours—you sleep up there!"
I change my clothes and climb in bed—
And bump into a pig named Fred.

Fred's asleep and will not budge.
His face is smeared with chocolate fudge.
All night long, I hear him wheeze.
He hogs the blankets while I freeze.

In the morning, right at dawn,
I get up and stretch and yawn.
And as we cruise along the coast
I eat jelly on my toast.

After breakfast I recline
Until aerobics class at nine.
The pigs prefer to exercise
While eating burgers, shakes, and fries.

A little later, by the pool,
The pigs are acting wicked cool.
They lie around on silly floats
And race their pudgy motorboats.

One pig's covered with tattoos
Depicting all the latest news.
Another jumps into the air
And splashes water everywhere.

In the boiler room below
(Where pigs are not supposed to go),
They're down there pounding on the pipes
And painting pink and purple stripes.

To get the furnace burning bright,
They fill it full of anthracite.
When Captain Krutch comes in to check,
Those naughty pigs run up on deck.

Tonight we'll dine with Captain Krutch.
The pigs don't like him very much.
He yells at them and calls them names
And messes up their piggy games.

I tell those pigs, "Now don't be rude.
Please use your forks and chew your food.
Just mind your manners when you eat
And do your best to keep things neat."

They come to dinner dressed divine;
Salute the Captain in a line.
The Captain scowls and, as he sits,
To his left a piggy spits.

A waiter brings us bowls of chowder.
The slurping starts and just gets louder.
The Captain frowns—he looks upset.
His glass gets tipped, his sleeve's all wet.

The table's soon piled high with food.
(The Captain's in an angry mood.)
A piggy swings a French bread bat
And knocks a meatball toward his hat.

The Captain rises from his chair—
A piggy pelts him with a pear.
Then the Captain, blind with rage,
Trips—and falls onto the stage.

He knocks the sultry singer down.
The singer shrieks, "You soiled my gown!"
The piggies help her to her feet
And twirl her to a mambo beat.

The piggies slide, and then they slip.
I hear the singer's gown go *r-r-rip!*
She gives our tablecloth a tug,
And all the food lands on the rug.

She wraps the cloth around her tight
And leaves the dining room in fright.
The pigs pursue her through the doors
While close behind the Captain roars.

All along the deck they run—
The pigs are having lots of fun!
The singer leads—she's moving fast.
The pigs are next, the Captain's last.

Some sailors catch them, one by one,
And scold those pigs for what they've done.
They load them in a little boat.
(I'm amazed the thing can float.)

Those pigs are such a jolly bunch.
They call, "Hey, Captain, let's do lunch!"
They try to splash him, then they snort.
I hope they make it back to port.

Without those pigs, this trip's a bore;
I lie around on deck and snore.
The days drag on, and then it's done.
I wish it could have been more fun.

When at last the cruise is through,
I head for home—I'm feeling blue.
But as I open up my door,
I notice something on the floor.

Leaning up against the wall,
A boat is anchored in the hall.
"Pigs ahoy!" I loudly shout.
And all those pigs come tumbling out.

I'm glad to see them, I confess,
Even though they've made a mess.
But cleaning up that mess can wait—

Right now we're going to celebrate!